Zelda and Ivy

ONE CHRISTMAS

Zelda and Ivy
ONE CHRISTMAS

LAURA MᶜGEE KVASNOSKY

CANDLEWICK PRESS
CAMBRIDGE, MASSACHUSETTS

To the
best gifts of all —
John, Timothy, & Noelle

Copyright © 2000 by Laura McGee Kvasnosky

First edition in this format 2006

The Library of Congress cataloged the original edition as follows:
Kvasnosky, Laura McGee.
Zelda and Ivy One Christmas / Laura McGee Kvasnosky. —1st ed.
p. cm.
Summary: After making a special Christmas gift for their elderly neighbor, two sisters find just what they wanted under their tree.
ISBN 0-7636-1000-3 (hardcover)
[1. Foxes—Fiction. 2. Sisters—Fiction. 3. Christmas—Fiction. 4. Neighbors—Fiction.] I. Title.
PZ7.K975 Zek   2000
[Fic]—dc21   99-046810

ISBN 0-7636-3047-0 (reformatted paperback)

10 9 8 7 6 5 4 3 2 1

Printed in Singapore

This book was typeset in Galliard and hand-lettered by the author-illustrator. The illustrations were done in gouache resist.

Candlewick Press
2067 Massachusetts Avenue
Cambridge, Massachusetts 02140

visit us at www.candlewick.com

CONTENTS

Chapter One
CHRISTMAS WISHES

One frosty morning, Zelda and Ivy helped
their neighbor Mrs. Brownlie bake ginger-
bread cookies.

"Christmas is almost here," said Mrs.
Brownlie. "What do you hope Santa
will bring?"

"A Princess Mimi doll," said Ivy quickly. "With the pink tutu and all the ballet accessories."

Zelda scratched her head. "I'm still deciding," she said.

While the cookies were baking, Mrs. Brownlie took out a Christmas catalog. "Maybe this will help," she said.

Ivy pulled out the craft box. "I'll string
the beads," she said.

"No," said Zelda. "You get the glitter
ready."

"I'll sprinkle the glitter," said Ivy.

"Let's put it under our tree until Christmas," said Ivy.

"I was just going to do that," said Zelda. "But you can if you really want to."

Later, when Ivy wasn't looking, Zelda moved the present close to her favorite ornament.

Chapter Two
CHRISTMAS FORTUNES

Zelda balanced a golden Christmas ornament on the birdbath and wrapped her muffler around her head like a turban.

"I am the Amazing Zeldarina," she said. "I can read the future in this magic ball."

"Okay," said Ivy. "What will Santa bring me for Christmas?"

Zelda looked into the ball. "I see a fox. Tall, orange, and handsome. You will marry him and have three babies named Bobo, Walter, and Polly."

"Come on," said Ivy. "Tell me about Christmas."

"You will journey far, to Zanzibar and
Zamboanga," answered Zelda.

"Oh boy," said Ivy. "But will Santa Claus bring me a Princess Mimi doll with the pink tutu and all the ballet accessories?"

Zelda looked thoughtful. "I see a glimmer of a velvet gown," she said.

"That's probably for you," said Ivy.

"Of course," said Zelda. She lifted her muzzle. "For the Christmas Ball."

"Do you see anything for me?" asked Ivy.

Zelda leaned in close. Just then the sweet smell of apple pie drifted up the street.

Ivy stood and looked deeply into the
ornament. She thought—she really
thought—she saw a Princess Mimi doll.

Chapter Three
CHRISTMAS gifts

"Let's pretend we're sisters," said Ivy.

"We are sisters," said Zelda.

"I know, but it's more fun to pretend," said Ivy. "And let's pretend we are lying in our beds on Christmas Eve, waiting for Santa."

"We are," said Zelda, yawning.

"And let's pretend Santa Claus brings me a Princess Mimi doll," said Ivy.

"Oh, all right," said Zelda. "As long as we pretend he brings me an evening gown."

Ivy was almost asleep when Zelda nudged her. "Go see what Santa left," she whispered.

"We can't go downstairs," said Ivy. "Not until morning."

"Come on," said Zelda. "Pretend to tiptoe down and look." She handed Ivy her slippers.

"Well, okay," said Ivy. "But I'm just pretending."

When Ivy came back, she looked sad.
"Santa hasn't come," she sniffed. "The
cookies we put out are still there."

"It must be too early," said Zelda.
"Let's go back to sleep."

"I can't sleep," said Ivy.

"Pretend," said Zelda.

On Christmas morning, two big boxes
from Santa Claus were next to the tree.
Boxes big enough to hold an evening gown
or a Princess Mimi doll. Zelda and Ivy
opened them eagerly to find . . .
matching bathrobes.

"This robe is
pure glamour,"
said Zelda.

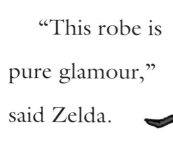

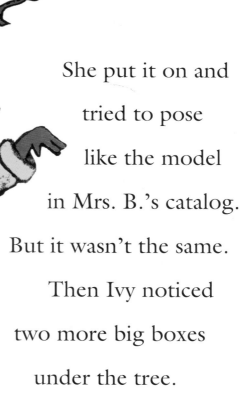

She put it on and
tried to pose
like the model
in Mrs. B.'s catalog.
But it wasn't the same.
Then Ivy noticed
two more big boxes
under the tree.

She crawled in for a closer look. "The tags say *To Zelda* and *To Ivy*," she read. "*Love, The Christmas Elf!*"

"Mine first," said Zelda. She tore off the wrapping. "Just what I wanted!" she shouted. Nestled in the tissue was a velvet gown, with gloves and a feather boa.

Next, Ivy carefully untaped the wrapping and slipped off the lid to her box. "Oh my," she whispered. "Princess Mimi!"

Zelda put on her new gown. "This is exactly like the one in Mrs. B.'s catalog," she said. "Let's go show her."

"Okay," said Ivy. "We can take her the present we made."

Zelda and Ivy knocked on Mrs. Brownlie's door. When she opened it, lovely Christmas music spilled onto the porch. "What a nice surprise," said Mrs. B. "Come in!"

Zelda handed Mrs. Brownlie the gift.

"The Christmas Elves left this under our

tree," explained Ivy.

Mrs. Brownlie unwrapped the gift and

held the new bracelet up to the light.

"This," she said, "is so snazzy! How

did the Christmas Elves know exactly

what I wanted?"

Zelda and Ivy grinned.

"A Christmas Elf

brought us just what we

wanted, too," said Ivy.

"See my Princess Mimi?"

"Pleased to meet you,

Princess Mimi," said Mrs. B.

"And this is my new

gown," said

Zelda, twirling.

"That looks like

a dancing dress, all

right," said Mrs.

Brownlie.

She turned up the music, then held out

one paw to Zelda and the other to Ivy.

"Shall we dance?" she asked.

They waltzed and whirled like snowflakes.

"You know," said Ivy. "This is like having our own Christmas Ball."

"That's just what I was thinking," said Zelda.

When the music ended, they all curtsied.

"Merry Christmas," said Zelda and Ivy.

"Yes," said Mrs. Brownlie. "A very merry Christmas!"